SAM WU

is <u>NOT</u> afraid of SHARKS

EGMONT

We bring stories to life

First published in Great Britain in 2018
by Egmont UK Limited
The Yellow Building, 1 Nicholas Road, London W11 4AN

ISBN 978 1 4052 8752 4

www.egmont.co.uk

A CIP catalogue record for this title is available from the British Library

67431/001

SAM WU

is NOT afraid of

SHARKS

This is TOTALLY fine

KATIE & KEVIN TSANG

Illustrated by Nathan Reed

EGMONT

TO OUR SIBLINGS:
JACK, JANE AND STEPHANIE

-Katie & Kevin Tsang

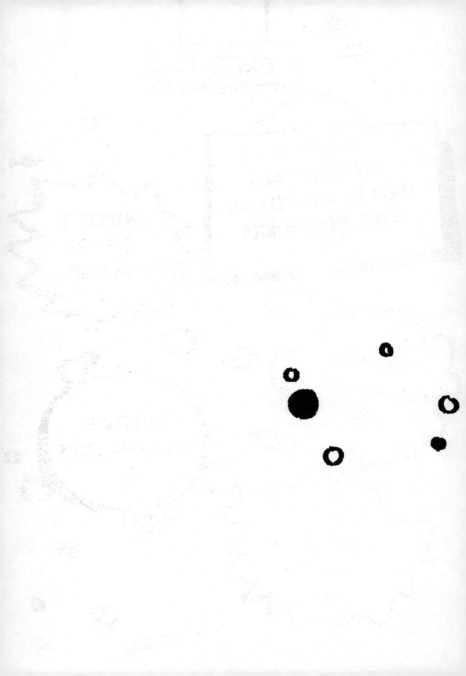

CONTENTS

CHAPTER 1

MY HISTORY AS A CERTIFIED, DEFINITELY NOT AFRAID GHOST-HUNTER

My name is **Sam Wu** and I am <u>**NOT**</u> afraid of sharks. Or ghosts. Or anything else, no matter what a certain someone — that someone being **Ralph Philip Zinkerman the Third** — might tell you. And whatever anyone tells you, I am <u>**NOT**</u> Scaredy-Cat Sam.

You might have heard about my adventures with some ghosts. They started

in the **Space Museum**

and then everything snowballed from there.[1]

Anyway, I've established that I'm **NOT** afraid of ghosts. **NOT** even the Ghost King, who is the number one bad guy in the entire universe. I know this from my favourite show,

There was a ghost in my house and we — that's me and my friends Zoe and Bernard — had to find it and chase it out of my house.

---

[1] I recently realized that when people say 'snowballed' they don't really mean an actual snowball like you'd throw at an enemy. They mean an AVALANCHE. Which sounds terrifying. **NOT** that I'm afraid of avalanches.

See, totally <u>NOT</u> scared!

True story.[2] We even have the ghost-hunter certificates to prove it.

Back to me being brave.

GHOST HUNTERS

---

[2] This story might <u>**NOT**</u> be 100 per cent true, but don't tell Ralph Philip Zinkerman that. Or his twin sister Regina.

I'm so brave that my sidekick is an actual, genuine, man-eating snake named **Fang.**[3]

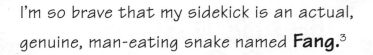

I thought that by proving I wasn't afraid of ghosts nobody would call me Scaredy-Cat Sam any more. I was wrong.

It was just the beginning of proving how **<u>NOT</u>** afraid I am.

[3] Fang doesn't actually have fangs, and I've also never seen him eat a man, but that isn't important. The important thing is that Fang is an actual snake and he's my very scary sidekick. **<u>NOT</u>** scary to me, scary to everyone else. Except to my little sister Lucy, who is apparently not afraid of anything.

CHAPTER 2

ONE FISH, TWO FISH

After the **INCIDENT** at the Space Museum,
which won't be spoken of (it involved me, an

Astro Blast Simulator
and a change of
trousers), I had to
prove my **bravery**
by getting a snake
sidekick and
becoming a certified
ghost-hunter.

7

It's kind of a long story. All you need to know is that I proved how **BRAVE** I am.

But apparently, bravery is something you have to prove over and over again.

I thought everything would go back to normal and I'd never have to hear the words

'Scaredy-Cat Sam'

again. But then we had a school trip to the aquarium. And that was when things **really went wrong.**[4]

It should have been a perfect day. I wasn't 100 per cent sure what to expect at the aquarium, but my best friend Bernard swore it was going to be

---

[4] But not quite as wrong as they went at the Space Museum. Maybe I should stop going on school trips.

AMAZING.

Up until this point I'd had exactly three experiences with the deep sea:

1. On my favourite show, **SPACE BLASTERS**, there was once an episode where they flew to a water planet and met a flying space sea turtle named Stephanie. There was also an **Evil Shark Lord** who was in cahoots with the Ghost King[5]. It was a great episode. Most people would have found it **TERRIFYING**, but I was only a little bit scared.

---

[5] He's the number one-enemy in the universe, according to Captain Jane, Spaceman Jack and ME. But Evil Shark Lord is probably enemy number two.

2. The beaches in Hong Kong (where my family is from) very sensibly have shark nets. To keep out the sharks. My little sister Lucy wondered what would happen **if a shark got IN** the shark net, but I told her that was impossible.[6]

3. When I asked Na-Na (that's my grandma — she lives with us) what an aquarium was, she told me it was like **the big fish** tanks at the seafood restaurants in Chinatown, which we go to on special occasions. Na-Na always picks out a fish that is **STILL SWIMMING** in a fish tank for us to have for dinner. One time I named the fish, but then it came out on a plate, so I don't name the fish from the tank **ANY MORE.**

---

[6] It actually sounded very possible and EXTREMELY scary. But I didn't want to worry her so I put on a brave face. All part of being a big brother.

So I thought that the aquarium was going to be like a **giant fish tank** where you picked out your dinner. When I told Bernard and Zoe that their mouths dropped open.

'**EW!**' said Zoe.

I frowned. 'Zoe, you eat fish. Just yesterday you had **fish fingers** for lunch,' I said.

'That's different!' she spluttered. We were on the bus on our way to the aquarium.

'How?' I said.

'It just **IS!** Tell him, Bernard,' she said.

Bernard frowned and then took out his thinking glasses. He only wears them when he is thinking **VERY HARD.**

'Well,' he said. 'Fish fingers come in a box. So obviously it is a completely different thing.'

'Yeah!' said Zoe. 'And fish don't even have fingers.'

'Exactly! Why are they called fish fingers?' I said, wiggling my own fingers.

'**I don't know**,' Zoe said loudly (the more unsure about something she is, the louder she gets). **They just are. But I do know you don't eat the fish at the aquarium.**'

I shrugged. 'Try telling Na-Na that.'

And then we arrived at the aquarium.

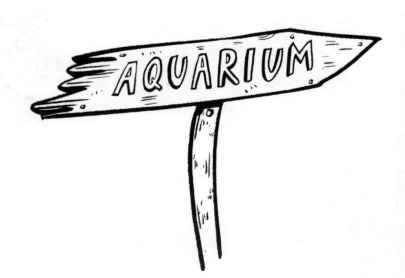

CHAPTER 3

ALIEN ENCOUNTER

From the outside, the aquarium looked a lot like the Space Museum. It was a **BIG** building and we had to queue up to go inside.

'Hey, Sam Wu-ser,' someone further back said with a snort. 'Do you have a stupid outfit for the aquarium too?'

It was Ralph. Only Ralph thinks it's **hilarious** to call me Sam Wu-ser because it rhymes with loser. And only Ralph snorts like that. I took a deep breath and tried to remember what my dad had said to do about Ralph. His advice was:

'Just ignore him.'

NOT that easy!

Ignoring Ralph is

Ralph pushed his way up through the queue until he was right behind me. He started poking me in the back. 'Hey! Hey! Sam Wu-ser! I'm talking to you! Hey! Hey!'

This was, as you might imagine, very hard to ignore.

'He doesn't have his SPACE BLASTERS outfit on because we're going to the aquarium not the Space Museum!' said Zoe.

 'OBVIOUSLY.'

I was, in fact, wearing a **SPACE BLASTERS** T-shirt, because it is the **best show ever**. I made it myself. And in honour of the aquarium trip, I'd even drawn on **space turtle** Stephanie. I didn't feel the need to point this out though.

Ralph was quiet for all of **FIVE SECONDS**. But then he barrelled on.

17

'Hey. Hey, Sam. I heard there is a submarine simulator in there. Bet you are too **scared** to get in it. Especially after what happened at the **Space Museum**.' He started laughing, but it wasn't a real laugh, it was some sort of pretend villain laugh. Then he pushed past me, because Ralph always pushes in queues, and went to the front.

'I'd like to put him in a submarine simulator,' Zoe muttered. 'And send it to the **BOTTOM OF THE SEA!**'

'Yeah!' said Bernard. Then he patted me on the shoulder. 'Don't listen to him, Sam. Everyone has forgotten about—'

'Don't say it!' I said. 'We don't talk about it,

REMEMBER?'

'Sorry!' said Bernard. Then he coughed. 'But, um, you aren't going to get into the submarine simulator, are you?'

'Bernard might have a point,' said Zoe, **tugging on her ponytail**.

'I wasn't planning to,' I said. 'But please can we stop taking about it?'

They nodded. Spaceman Jack, my favourite character on **SPACE BLASTERS**, never has to deal with this kind of thing. He **NEVER** does anything embarrassing, but if he did, his friends would definitely **NEVER** bring it up.

'Come along, you three, **hurry up!**' It was our teacher, Ms Winkleworth. 'We have lots to see – and we don't want to be late for the feeding at the shark tank!'

THE FEEDING?
AT THE WHAT?
WHAT KIND OF FEEDING?
WHO IS FEEDING WHO WHAT?

Before I had a chance to think about all the ways a live shark-feeding was more than a little **dangerous**, we were shuffled into the aquarium.

It was *nothing* like the fish tanks in Chinatown.

'See, Sam! How **COOL** is this?' Bernard waved his arms around. I tried to look at everything all at once but it was impossible.

It was as if we were **underwater** but somehow breathing air. It was like being on **a spaceship in water** – dark and filled with aliens! Luckily, I have lots of experience with aliens from watching **SPACE BLASTERS** so I was **TOTALLY** fine. But otherwise I might have been a tiny bit afraid.

'That thing isn't a fish,'
I spluttered, pointing at this **HUGE
PURPLE BLOB** that was somehow
floating above my head. I could hear Captain
Jane (she's the captain of TUBS, **The
Universe's Best Spacecraft**) in my head,
telling me to take a deep breath and stay calm.
'What IS that?'

'**It's a jellyfish!**' said Zoe. Her eyes were huge.

'LIKE THE POISONOUS KIND?' I said in a very calm but also very loud way.

'Yep! That's right,' said a friendly voice from above me. I looked up. It was someone who worked at the aquarium. Her name tag said '**Betty**'. 'That is a jellyfish! One of forty-eight species we've got here in the aquarium.'

'**Ohhhh!**' said Zoe and Bernard and everyone else. They all seemed way too excited about the fact that we were now trapped underwater, surrounded by **POISONOUS JELLYFISH**.

'Mmmmm,' I said, nodding as if I too was excited. 'But, Zoe,' I whispered, 'what if it gets out?'

'It can't get out!' she whispered back. We'd been pushed forwards **till our noses were almost touching the glass**.

'That's what we thought about Fang!' I said in a louder whisper. 'And we were pretty **wrong** about that!'

As I've told you, Fang is my

FIERCE SNAKE

sidekick. He escaped
from his tank once. With
the help of Butterbutt,
my sister's cat. **It's
kind of a long story**.
But the point is, he wasn't
supposed to get out of
his cage and he did. So I
didn't think Zoe could blame me
for being a little . . . antsy[7] about
the possibility of **super-dangerous**
creatures escaping from their cages.

'That was totally different!' she said. 'And
anyway, Butterbutt isn't here.'

'**You never know with Butterbutt**,'
I muttered darkly.

---

[7] Antsy but definitely **NOT** scared.

25

'Okay, everyone,' said Betty the guide, leading us over to what looked like a pool of **sea monsters**, 'it's time for the petting tank! Everyone is going to get a turn to touch some of their favourite sea creatures. **We've got starfish, sea slugs and stingrays!** Who wants to go first?'

I stared at Aquarium Guide Betty. 'Touch . . . a stingray?' Didn't Betty hear herself? It says **STING** in the name! Who would want to touch a **STING**ray? That's like asking, 'Who wants to pet this **SPIKY** porcupine? Or this **POISONOUS** scorpion?'

'We've got a volunteer!' said Betty. She reached out and pulled me forwards.

'**Sam won't do it!**' Ralph said with a snort. 'He's too scared.'

'**No he's not!**' said Zoe. 'Right, Sam?'

'Right,' I said. I tried to smile bravely but my mouth wasn't really working.

And then

Betty took

my hand and

put it on a

I was totally <u>NOT</u> scared!!

STINGRAY!

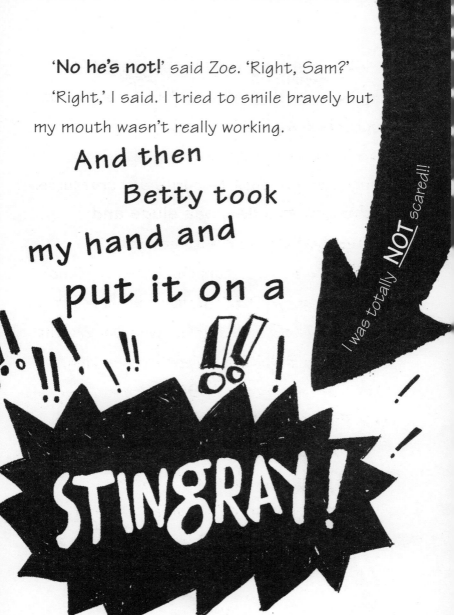

It was **rubbery** and slimy and **VERY** unpleasant. It felt deadly. And I wasn't even touching the stinger!

My whole class gasped.

Bernard gave me a thumbs-up. I really hoped the stingray didn't decide to, you know, **STING ME**.

'You all right?' said Betty. 'You seem to be a bit shaky.'

'I'm fine! Fine!' I said. 'The water is just . . . cold. **Really cold**. Brrr!'

Betty raised her eyebrows. 'It's room temperature.'

'**SO COLD**,' I said. I wanted to pull my hand out of the water but I didn't know how to do it without everyone noticing.

'Um, it is probably **someone else's turn**,' I said.

'I want to try!' It was Regina, Ralph's twin sister. She isn't awful like he is.

29

She is actually kind of nice. **She also doesn't snort as much**. Actually, I don't think I've ever heard her snort even once.

'Well, come on up!' said Betty, who still hadn't let go of my hand.

Regina **SQUEEZED** in next to me and put her hand straight into the water. 'This is so cool,' she said, grinning at me.

'Oh yeah,' I said casually. '**Super cool**.' Then Betty let go of my hand and I whipped it out of the water so fast that I splashed Regina.

DO NOT FEED THE FISH!

'**Sorry!**' I said.

She laughed. 'That's okay! It's just water.'

Just **STINGRAY-INFESTED WATER**, I thought, but I just nodded as if I wasn't at all worried about the contents of the water.

I turned around and gave Zoe and Bernard **a big grin**.

No more Scaredy-Cat Sam here! Spaceman Jack and Captain Jane would have been **proud.**

CHAPTER 4

EVIL SHARK LORDS

Now that I'd obviously done the **BRAVEST** thing anyone could do at the aquarium, I felt much more relaxed.

'**That was great!**' I said to Bernard as we made our way through the rest of the aquarium. 'Did you see me **wrangle** that stingray?'

Bernard blinked. 'You mean when the guide put your hand in the water?'

'I touched it too!' said Zoe.

'Yeah, but I think the one I touched was the **scariest** one,' I said. 'Definitely the ringleader of the group.'

'I don't think stingrays have leaders,' said Bernard.

'These ones do,' I said. '**I could just tell**.'

Bernard frowned. 'I'll have to look it up later.' Bernard loves to look things up. It is kind of his **superpower** – being smart and knowing facts. Zoe's super power is being super fast. My super power is being **SUPER BRAVE**, obviously.

We turned the corner and in front of us was the biggest tank we'd seen yet. **THE SHARK TANK.**

Maybe the stingrays weren't the scariest thing in the aquarium.

'Gather in close,' said Betty. 'But tdon't rap on the glass – we don't want to bother the sharks.'

'**Of course** we don't want to bother the sharks,' I said to Zoe. 'Who would want to bother **A SHARK?**

Then I saw who was rapping on the glass. Ralph. Of course. If anyone was going to annoy a shark it would be him.

'Did you know that **sharks are older than dinosaurs?**' said tour-guide Betty. 'They've been around for over **FOUR HUNDRED MILLION YEARS.**'

Bernard gasped. As I said, he loves facts. He raised his hand. 'Does that mean that they are like dinosaurs that live in the sea?'

'**Kind of!**' said Betty. 'But unlike the dinosaurs, they've managed to survive all these years. **Masters of survival!**'

And then I saw one. My very first shark sighting. It was <u>**NOT**</u> going to be my last.

It looked just like the sharks in the movies but **BIGGER** and **MEANER**. It had big black eyes and rows and rows of **razor-sharp** teeth. And I was sure it was looking right at me.

'Whoa,' said Zoe.

'Whoa,' said Bernard.

I didn't say anything. I couldn't believe that I was staring at a **REAL LIVE SHARK**. Which could **EAT ME**.

A few other sharks swam by too, but the first one — the one staring me down — was definitely the scariest one. <u>**NOT**</u> that I was scared of it. But everyone else probably was because it was a **very scary shark**.

'And we arrived **just in time** for the feeding!' said Betty.

Oh no! The **FEEDING!** With all of the excitement, I'd forgotten about the **FEEDING**.

Ralph cheered. 'This is going to **be the best!**' he said to his friends. 'I can't wait to see the shark **DESTROY** something.' Then **he bared his teeth like a shark.**

'Ralph,' said Regina. 'Please calm down.' But she looked excited too. Everyone looked excited. I didn't get it! How could you be excited when we still didn't know **WHAT** or WHO was going to get fed to the sharks?

In one episode of SPACE BLASTERS they went to **Shark Planet**, which was run by the **Evil Shark Lord**, and he almost tricked

Spaceman Jack into being his dinner!

Doesn't everyone know that sharks are evil masterminds? How else do you think they have survived for **MILLIONS AND MILLIONS** of years?

The sharks were **swimming faster** now – all of them except the big one. The big one just kept moving in slow circles, going slower every time it passed **me, Zoe and Bernard**. It was looking at me. I was sure of it. Every time it swam by, its **eyes fixed on me**. Even Bernard said, 'Why is that shark looking at us?'

'It's not looking at us,' scoffed Zoe. 'How can you even tell what it's looking at? Its eyes are on either side of its head! **It's looking everywhere!**'

'Well, if it is looking everywhere then that also means it is looking at us,' said Bernard. 'So I'm technically right.'

'**The shark isn't looking at us**,' repeated Zoe.

And then, as if the shark was **LISTENING** (which it probably was, because, as I said, they are **SNEAKY MASTERMINDS**), it slowly turned and came right at us!

We all took a step back from the tank. Even Zoe.

'Now can you admit it is looking at us?' I whispered.

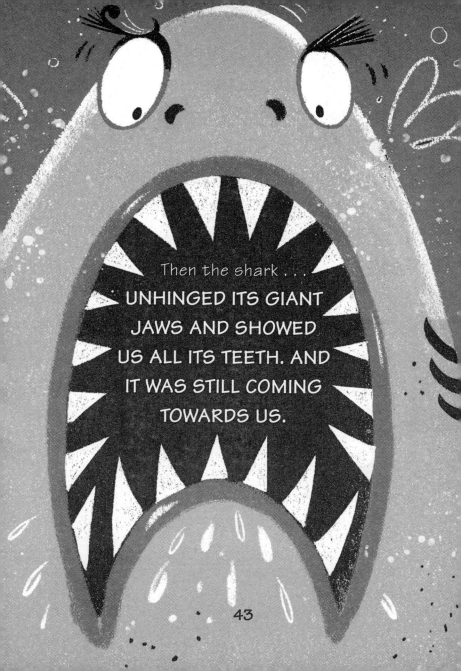

Then the shark . . .
UNHINGED ITS GIANT
JAWS AND SHOWED
US ALL ITS TEETH. AND
IT WAS STILL COMING
TOWARDS US.

43

'What . . . **what is it doing?**' said
Bernard. He sounded a little shaky. 'Excuse
me! Excuse me! Is that normal shark
behaviour?'

Betty came over. 'Oh, don't you worry!
That shark there is just **CRAZY CHARLIE**.
He's our **biggest** and **moodiest** shark. He's
also the most vain. Crazy Charlie just likes
to show off his teeth before he eats. He's
very proud of them.'

'Why . . . why is he called Crazy Charlie?'
I asked. This all seemed **highly dangerous**.

Betty shrugged. 'Oh, Charlie is
just a bit . . . **unpredictable**. He follows
his own schedule and is a really picky
eater. Sometimes he doesn't eat at all
during **feeding time**. And other times,

he'll scare the rest of the sharks away and eat **all the fish** himself!'

By this time Crazy Charlie had passed us and was making another round. But still, every time he swam by, I was sure he was looking **STRAIGHT AT ME** – staring me down and sizing me up.

'Look!' said Regina, pointing upwards. **We all looked up** and saw chunks of . . . something falling from the top of the tank.

'What **IS** that?' said Bernard.

'**Special shark food**' said Betty. 'Frozen fish with multivitamins stuffed inside them! Keeps the sharks healthy and **strong**.'

'Frozen fish?' said Zoe. '**LIKE FISH FINGERS?**'

'Not quite,' said our guide with a smile. 'But close. I bet our **sharks** would like fish fingers too.'

'Told you that you could get fish fingers at an aquarium,' I whispered to Zoe.

Betty walked away to answer someone else's question. **All of the sharks were swimming** to the top of the tank to get their lunch.

All of them but one. **CRAZY CHARLIE**. He was still swimming in slow circles, coming **closer** and **closer** to us with every loop.

46

'He reminds me of something,' I said, watching him. 'It's as if he's **mind-controlling** all the other sharks!'

'Sharks don't have mind control,' said Zoe.

'Some do! Like the Evil Shark Lord on SPACE BLASTERS,' I said. 'He controls ALL the sharks on Shark Planet.'

'Sam, we've been over this. Just because something happens on SPACE BLASTERS, does not mean it's real,' said Zoe.

'It might be,' I said.

'Maybe, but **you don't have any proof**,' said Zoe.

I pointed at the **giant, crazy shark** swimming in front of us. 'Proof! Doesn't that shark look **EXACTLY** like the Evil Shark Lord? They have got to be related.'

'Related **HOW?**' said Bernard, who always wants to know the details.

'I don't know!' I shrugged. 'They are probably cousins or something.'

Everyone else in the class was watching the sharks eating their **special shark lunch** – everyone but me, Zoe and Bernard, who couldn't take our eyes off **CRAZY CHARLIE.**

He couldn't take his eyes off us either.

'I guess he is acting **kind of weird**,' admitted Zoe.

'There has to be a scientific explanation,' said Bernard.

'Yes, there is! **HE WANTS TO EAT US**,' I said.

'Even if he wanted to eat us, he wouldn't be able to,' said Bernard, logical as always. 'I mean, unless he **JUMPED OUT** of the tank or broke the glass. And that's impossible.'

Just then, **CRAZY CHARLIE** came around on another loop. But this time he didn't keep on swimming past. He turned towards us, as he had before, **opened his mouth** and **CHARGED AT ME**. I thought I was going to **die**. It was like my encounter with the

Ghost King all over again.

'Argh!' I said, falling backwards.

'Argh!' said Zoe and Bernard because I'd fallen on them.

'ARGH!' said everyone else who had just seen CRAZY CHARLIE ram his head into the glass.

I closed my eyes, waiting for the glass to shatter, the water to **pour over us** and the end to come.

51

It didn't.

Instead . . .

Laughter.

I opened my eyes and saw Ralph Philip Zinkerman standing over me, **pointing** and **LAUGHING**. The tank was still intact behind him, and **CRAZY CHARLIE** was nowhere to be seen.

'Scaredy-Cat Sam is scared of sharks!'

Ralph laughed.

Oh no. <u>**NOT**</u> this again.

At least I hadn't **wet my pants** like I did at the Space Museum.

But don't <u>EVER</u> mention that!

It only happened **once**. And I was obviously getting **braver** by the day.

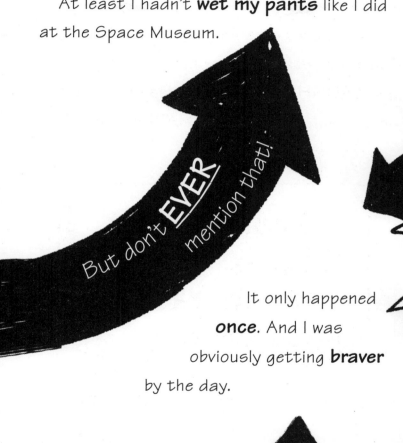

CHAPTER 5

A DANGEROUS INVITATION

I thought everyone was going to **make fun of me** the next day at school, but luckily there was something happening to distract them all.

'**Did you hear?**' Zoe whispered to me from her desk. 'Ralph and Regina are having a **HUGE** birthday party at the beach next weekend!'

'At the **beach?**' I couldn't imagine why anyone would want to have a party at a beach, home of **ALL THE SHARKS**.

Especially after what had happened at the aquarium. Hadn't everyone else seen **CRAZY CHARLIE** try to **eat** me?

'Yes! They are passing out invitations today!'

I frowned. 'Ralph doesn't like me at all,' I said. 'There's **NO WAY** I'm invited to his birthday.'

'Don't be silly! They are inviting the **WHOLE** class! I heard Regina telling someone.'

I wondered if they were going to invite the whole class but me. **I wouldn't put it past Ralph**. I had to say something to show that I didn't care if I was invited or not.

Even though **I did care**. I didn't want to miss a party that the whole class was going to.

'Well, even if they invited me, I don't think it

would be a **good idea to go**, because of the sharks and everything,' I said.

Zoe shook her head. '**Sharks don't go on land**, Sam. You can go to the beach without getting in the sea.'

'Zoe, did you even watch that Shark Planet episode of SPACE BLASTERS? Sharks are **VERY** sneaky! You should know this after what happened yesterday.'

'**Hey, Sam**,' someone said right in front of my desk. It was Regina. She was holding a basket full of envelopes.

'**Next weekend is mine** and Ralph's birthday party. I hope you can come!' She held out an envelope with **MY NAME** on it. 'And you too, Zoe!'

Zoe and I took our invites. On the front was a friendly cartoon shark holding out a cake.

Come make a splash at Ralph and Regina's beach birthday bash!

12–5 pm

Big Wave Beach
Lunch and cake
will be served

Don't forget your
swimsuit!

'Thanks, Regina!' I said. 'This looks
PRETTY . . . COOL.'

'So you can come?'

'Um,' I said. **'I'll have to ask my mum.'**
I didn't want to commit to anything yet.
Especially <u>**NOT**</u> to something that was
clearly so **dangerous**.

'Well, I hope she says yes! It's going to be
a **really fun** party,' said Regina. 'I have to
give these out to everyone else.' She turned
and went to the next row of desks.

'**See**.' I held up the invitation to Zoe.
'There's even a shark on the invitation. **Why
would anyone want to have a birthday
party with a shark?'**

Zoe just rolled her eyes. 'Sam, we **can't**
miss this birthday party! It is going to be

the **BEST!** At their birthday last year they had a magician, a piñata and a cake that was **TALLER THAN ME!'**

I shrugged. 'That sounds okay, I guess.' I've never had a **big birthday party**. I always celebrate by having special birthday noodles with my family. Na-Na has an **ancient family recipe** that is delicious. The best noodles ever! And my mum makes me my favourite dessert, Chinese egg tarts.

I started thinking that maybe this year I'd invite Zoe and Bernard over. I knew I couldn't ever invite the **ENTIRE CLASS.** But if I *could*, I'd have a big SPACE BLASTERS-themed party! It would be the **best birthday party ever**.

Part of me, **a really tiny part**, was a little jealous that Ralph and Regina got to have such a big party. I'd never even known I wanted to have my own **BIG BIRTHDAY PARTY** until right this minute.

'Well, let's discuss it with Bernard,' said Zoe.

At break, we met Bernard at our usual spot by the fence.

'Did you get an invitation to Ralph and Regina's birthday party?' I asked.

Bernard nodded but **he looked glum**.

'What's wrong?' said Zoe.

'It's at the beach,' Bernard said.

Zoe threw her hands up in the air. 'Not you too! What's wrong with the beach? The beach is great! **I LOVE THE BEACH!**'

'**What's wrong with the beach?** What **ISN'T** wrong with the beach?' I held out my hand to count.

ONE: SHARKS!

TWO: JELLYFISH!

THREE: CRABS!

FOUR: WAVES!

'**Definitely waves**,' said Bernard, who looked paler than ever.

'I could go on and on,' I said, 'but **WHO**

has time for that?'

'So we aren't going?' said Bernard
hopefully.

'Oh no,' I said grimly, 'we have to go.
Otherwise **everyone will think we are
scared!**'

'You ARE scared,' said Zoe.

I glared at her. 'I'm <u>**NOT**</u>.'

'If you say so,' she said. **'I'm definitely <u>NOT</u> scared**. Like I said, I love the beach! We'll have fun.'

Bernard buried his face in his hands. **'I've never even been to the beach!'** he moaned.

'Then we have to go!' said Zoe. 'It's fun. I promise!'

'We can't just go **willy-nilly**,' I said. It's a phrase I learned from SPACE BLASTERS. Captain Jane always says it when Spaceman Jack does something without thinking. **'WE NEED A PLAN!'** I did what I always do when faced with a problem. I thought about the last episode of SPACE BLASTERS I'd seen. The Evil Shark Lord had returned, and the

64

SPACE BLASTERS crew knew they had to battle him in his home turf – **UNDERWATER!**

To prepare for it, Captain Jane took TUBS to a safer water planet, and **they practised their space-ninja moves** underwater while wearing their special underwater spacesuits. We needed our own test run. 'I'll ask Na-Na to take us **to the beach** this weekend,' I said. 'So we can be prepared.'

'**PERFECT!**' said Zoe.

'There's one catch though,' I said.

'What is it?' said Bernard.

'You know Na-Na – she'll take us to the beach, but only if we weed her garden.'

'**Not again!**' said Bernard.

CHAPTER 6

SHARKS DON'T LIVE ON THE MOON

As I suspected, we were able to bribe Na-Na to take us to the **beach** in exchange for weeding her garden.[8]

---

[8]Weeding a garden is much more dangerous than you would think. Especially since Na-Na started growing SUPER-HOT CHILLI PEPPERS that can probably burn your face off.

What I **WASN'T** expecting was for my little sister Lucy to want to come too. And for Na-Na to let her. Lucy didn't even have to help weed the garden!

'This isn't just **a fun trip to the beach!** This is a **VERY** serious reconnaissance mission!' I said as **I stuffed my backpack** full of snacks in the kitchen.

Lucy **scrunched up** her face. 'What's rec-onn-aiss-ance?' she said.

'It's when you go on a **SECRET MISSION** to gather information so your enemies don't catch you unawares!' I said, puffing out my chest a little bit. I'd learned it on **SPACE BLASTERS**. **Even Bernard** hadn't known what it meant.

Lucy laughed. 'Sam, you **DON'T** have

any enemies!'

'You are **just too little to** understand,' I said, patting her on the head.

Lucy rolled her eyes and picked up her cat, Butterbutt. 'You're so weird,' she said. 'And I'm coming on the **SPY MISSION** too. I'm a **super spy!**' She twirled in a circle, making Butterbutt yowl.

I hate to admit it, but **she was right**. After all, she had been the one who'd helped us figure out where **my snake Fang** was hiding when he went missing.

'Fine,' I said. 'But it's **MY** secret mission! You are just a **junior spy**. You have to do what we say.'

Lucy laughed again. 'I never do what you say,' she said.

It's true. She might be **the little sister**, but Lucy doesn't let **ANYONE** boss her around.

'Why didn't anyone tell me that the sand would be **so scratchy?**' said Bernard, hopping back and forth.

'Well, we can go and rinse it off in the water,' said Zoe, **pointing** at the blue sea up ahead of us.

'<u>**NO!**</u>' Bernard and I said at the same time.

'That's the whole reason we're here, isn't

it?' said Zoe. 'To get familiar with **this beach** so we are prepared for the party?'

'We can do that without **GOING IN THE WATER**,' I said. I reached into my backpack and pulled out a pair of binoculars. **'We've got everything we need right here**.'

'Nobody is going anywhere until you all have sun cream on,' said Na-Na. She was putting up our **BIG UMBRELLA**. 'Now get over here and hold still.' Na-Na always makes sure we wear sun cream. After she had slathered us in it, we sat in the sand and **plotted**.

'Sand is so . . . **SANDY**,' said Bernard with a frown.

Considering he's the smartest kid in our class, I was surprised by how not-smart he was being about the beach. He was really out of his element.

'**Duh**,' said Zoe. She was wearing sunglasses and building a sandcastle. She seemed less interested in the spy mission. 'When do we get lunch?'

'**You both need to focus!**' I said. 'Sure, everything is fine with just us here, but **imagine** what it will be like next week with everyone. **ANYTHING** could happen! We need to make sure we are prepared for the worst.'

'**Fine**,' said Zoe. She was just finishing

the top of her **sandcastle**. 'And how do you suggest we prepare ourselves?'

'Excellent question.' I said. 'I was hoping someone would ask. First, before we can properly prepare, we need to know **EXACTLY** what we're dealing with here. My reconnaissance so far has told me that:

1. This beach is **BIG**. We need to make sure we stay close. Someone could easily get lost.
2. It's WINDY here. People seem to have a hard time keeping hats on their heads. Especially Na-Na.
3. Sun. There is a **LOT** of sun.
4. The sea is **even bigger** than the beach. It is going to be **VERY** hard to spot a shark. Even with my trusty binoculars.

'So what is our plan?' said Zoe.

'I haven't got that far yet,' I admitted. 'I was hoping one of you would have a good idea based **on ALL** of the information we have.'

'I think we need to test the water,' said Zoe, then she paused. 'Not like when Spaceman Jack says it and means they need to try something new. I think we need to **ACTUALLY** get into the water.'

'Well, **technically** that would also mean trying something new, so Spaceman Jack's use of it would still work,' I said. I always defend **Spaceman Jack**.

'I don't think we should get in the water,' said Bernard.

'Bernard, you have to know **there aren't any sharks!**' said Zoe.

'What do you mean there aren't any sharks!' I replied. '**OF COURSE THERE ARE SHARKS!** Where do you think they live? **THE MOON?** Sharks live in the sea! We shouldn't bother them. They don't come into our houses, so we shouldn't go into theirs.'

Zoe frowned. 'What about on that one episode of **SPACE BLASTERS**? Weren't there sharks on the moon?'

'I see what you are trying to do here,' I said. 'But it isn't going to work. I'm **NOT** getting in that water.'

Just then **something whizzed past me**, sending sand flying in my face.

'**Butterbutt!** Come back here!' cried Lucy, running after the blur of fur.

'Butterbutt? You brought **BUTTERBUTT**

to the beach?' I said, but Lucy was already too far away to hear me, racing down the beach . . . towards the water.

'Sam! Go and get your sister! And that stupid cat!' yelled Na-Na.

'RIGHT NOW.'

'**COME ON**, Sam!' said Zoe, jumping up and grabbing my hand. 'We have to save Butterbutt!'

'I'll stay here!' said Bernard. '**You guys go!**'

I wanted to ask him why he wasn't coming with us, but **there wasn't time**. Zoe was pulling me after her.

'Faster, Sam!' she said. Zoe is the **fastest** person in our **WHOLE** class, so it was impossible to keep up with her, but I did my best.

The closer we got to the water, the more **nervous** I felt.

'Can Lucy swim?' Zoe yelled over her shoulder at me.

'**I think so!**' I said, but I wasn't totally sure. She was wearing blow-up armbands. I suddenly felt like the **worst big brother in the world**. How did I <u>**NOT**</u> know if my little sister could swim? That was the kind of thing I should have known. I should have checked before we came to the beach! I ran faster, sweat pouring down my forehead and into my eyes.

'**Where'd she go?**' I shouted at Zoe. 'I can't see her!'

'She's gone around those rocks!' cried Zoe. 'Come on! **Faster!**'

I don't think I've ever run **SO** fast. I wasn't scared of sharks any more. I wasn't scared of anything. I had to catch up to my sister.

And her stupid cat.

Zoe went around **the rocks** and I chased after her. Just ahead I could see Lucy in her red swimsuit and **pigtails** and she was About to get in the water!

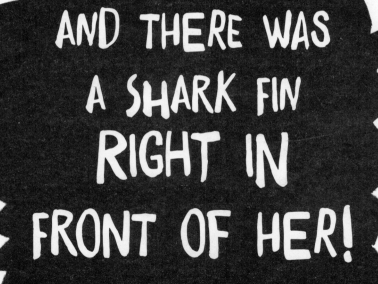

AND THERE WAS A SHARK FIN RIGHT IN FRONT OF HER!

'NO, LUCY!' I screamed as loud as I could and I ran even faster. **So fast** that I even passed Zoe.

Lucy turned back towards me, the **water** up to her ankles and the shark fin right behind her! She was holding **a squiggling Butterbutt** in her arms.

'I'm okay, Sam,' she said. 'Why are you yelling?'

'GET OUT OF THE WATER, LUCY!' I yelled. **'THERE'S A SHARK RIGHT BEHIND YOU!'**

'I'm not even in the water!' Lucy said, running up on the sand.

I was **so happy** she hadn't been eaten by a shark!

'Where is it? Where is the shark?' she said,

looking out at the sea.

At this point I was so **out of breath** from all my running and yelling that I couldn't even talk. Instead I just pointed at the fin that was still right in front of us!

'Oh my gosh! **HE'S RIGHT. THAT'S A SHARK!**' said Zoe.

'Are you sure?' said Lucy, still squinting at the sea.

'I don't want to stick around to find out!' said Zoe. '**COME ON!** Sam, you take Butterbutt!' She took Butterbutt out of Lucy's arms and thrust the cat at me, then took Lucy's hand.

Butterbutt yowled and scratched me. 'Why do I have to carry Butterbutt?' I said between gasping breaths.

But Zoe and Lucy had already gone around the rocks and couldn't hear me. I looked back out at the **water,** looking for the shark fin.

I couldn't see it. But I **knew** that didn't mean it was gone.

'I'm <u>NOT</u> afraid of you!' I yelled at the water.[9]

---
[9] This story might <u>NOT</u> be 100 per cent true, but don't tell Ralph Philip Zinkerman that. Or his twin sister Regina.

CHAPTER 7

BUTTERBUTT THE BEACH CAT

'You **didn't** see a shark,' said Na-Na. She was setting up a grill on the sand to cook our lunch.

'Yes, we did!' I said. 'Zoe, you tell her!'

'I think we saw a shark,' said Zoe.

'Yes, you **think** you did,' said Na-Na. 'There aren't sharks here.'

'I SAW A FIN!' I yelled. 'Those are **SHARK-INFESTED WATERS**.'

Na-Na looked up and sighed. 'Oh, Sam, you

have such a great imagination.'

'**I KNOW WHAT I SAW**. Tell her, Lucy!'

Lucy was sitting next to Na-Na, playing with Butterbutt in the sand. She shrugged. 'I didn't see **a shark**,' she said.

'That's because you don't know what a shark looks like! We just saw one at the aquarium. '

Bernard leaned towards me. 'Was it really a shark?' he said, eyes wide.

'**YES!**' I said.

Bernard's eyes got even wider.

Na-Na put some food on the grill. 'If you say so, Sam.' But then she looked up and smiled at me. '**Good job** going after Lucy,' she said. She turned and frowned at Lucy. 'You know not to run off like that,' she scolded.

'But I **had to** chase Butterbutt!' said Lucy.

'I can't believe you brought Butterbutt in your backpack!' I said. '**WHO BRINGS A CAT TO THE BEACH?**'

'Of course I brought Butterbutt! He's a **beach kitty**,' said Lucy, stroking Butterbutt behind the ears.

'He was almost **SHARK-FOOD KITTY**,' I said.

'Sam, stop scaring your sister,' said Na-Na.

'I'm **not scared!**' said Lucy.

Zoe eyed the grill. 'What . . . what exactly are you putting on there?' she said.

'**Squid!**' said Na-Na. 'I used to have grilled squid all the time back in Hong Kong.'

Bernard, who had been **pretty quiet** ever since we got back, nudged me. 'But we aren't in Hong Kong,' he said.

I sighed. 'Just try the squid,' I said. Ever since Zoe and Bernard came over to my house for dinner, tried my **favourite** dish[10] and liked it, they've been better about trying new food. But I can understand why they thought the squid looked weird. It did still have **tentacles**.

'Don't worry,' I added. 'We've also got hot dogs.'

<hr>

[10] Roast duck and turnip cake.

'Of course we have hot dogs!' said Na-Na. **'I love hot dogs!'**

'Thank **GOODNESS**,' said Zoe. Then she looked up at me and smiled. 'But I'll try the squid too.'

We sat in a circle in the sand eating our hot dogs, squid and corn on the cob.

'What do you think of the squid?' I asked.

Bernard poked his with a plastic fork. 'It looks . . .'

I tensed.

'It looks like **A SQUID**,' he said. 'Like one we saw at the aquarium.'

'Of course it looks like a squid!' said Na-Na. 'You don't want it to look like a squid? Give it to me.' She reached over and took

Bernard's plate out of his hands, then cut his **squid** into small pieces. 'Now it doesn't look like a squid. **Eat it.**'

Nobody says no to Na-Na.

Bernard looked at me and then took a bite. He chewed, and chewed some more.

'I know it's **a little** chewy,' I said apologetically. I should have never let Na-Na bring squid to a beach picnic with my friends.

'**I LIKE IT!**' Bernard declared.

'You do?' I said.

'You do?' said Zoe, who still hadn't touched her squid.

'Of course he does,' said Na-Na. 'You always say he's a **smart boy**.'

Bernard beamed.

'**I'm smart too!**' said Zoe, shovelling her squid into her mouth.

'Not **TOO** much!' I said, but Zoe was already chewing away.

'I like it too!' she said with her **mouth full of squid**.

Na-Na nodded approvingly, and I ate my own squid with a smile.

After lunch, while Zoe, Bernard and I were plotting what to do about the **SHARK**, Lucy came over and tapped Bernard on the shoulder.

'**Can you swim?**' she said.

'Of course he can swim,' I answered. Everyone I knew could swim.

'Obviously,' added Zoe.

'Um,' said Bernard.

'**WHAT?**' I said. 'You can't swim?'

'Shh! Keep it down! I don't want anyone to know!' said Bernard. 'It's embarrassing!'

'**I knew it!**' said Lucy. She really is an excellent spy.

'How did you know?' said Bernard.

'Because you didn't want to go in the water. And because I saw you try on my **armbands**.'

Bernard **BLUSHED**. 'Oh.'

'Wait,' said Zoe. 'You really can't swim?'

'Lots of people can't swim!' Bernard blustered.

'So that's why you didn't want to go in the water? Not **because of the shark?**' I asked.

'Statistically speaking,' said Bernard, because he **loves** to quote statistics, 'the chances of me – or any of you – drowning in the sea are much higher than any of us getting eaten by a shark.'

HIGHER
CHANCE

**STATS:
CAUSES OF DEATH**

LOWER
CHANCE

DROWNING   **EATEN BY A SHARK**

I frowned. 'I don't believe you,' I said. 'I'm an **EXCELLENT** swimmer.' I might have been exaggerating a *little* bit. By excellent swimmer, I meant I could **doggy-paddle**.

'Show-off,' muttered Bernard.

'Why don't you know how to swim?' asked Lucy.

Bernard shrugged. 'I never learned. **I was busy learning other things**. And my parents never took me to a pool or to a beach, so I never needed to know how to swim.' Then he looked anxious. 'Until now.'

'**It's okay**,' I said. 'We aren't going to go to the party anyway. Not just because of you, but because of the **SHARK**.'

'What? We aren't going to the birthday party?' said Zoe.

'**Nope**,' I said firmly. 'Between the shark sighting, and Bernard's situation . . .'

'You already didn't want to go! Don't blame me!' said Bernard. '**BLAME THE SHARK!**'

'Anyway, it's all too dangerous,' I said. 'As your friend, I can't let us go. As Captain Jane would say, **it's for the good of the ship**.'

'We aren't on a spaceship!' sputtered Zoe.

'Zoe,' I said seriously, leaning towards her. 'You saw that shark fin, right?'

She bit her lip. 'I think so.'

'Do YOU want to go swimming in **shark-infested waters?**'

She shook her head.

'Did you really see it too?' said Bernard.

'Yes,' admitted Zoe.

'Exactly! It would be **MADNESS** to go to this birthday party,' I said. 'So we're agreed?' I put my hand out for our signature **SPACE BLASTERS**' handshake.

'Agreed,' said Bernard, extending his hand.

'**But the piñata . . .**' said Zoe.

'**WOULD YOU SWIM WITH A SHARK FOR A PIÑATA?**'

I demanded.

'Okay, agreed,' said Zoe, putting her hand out too.

'**For the good of the ship!**' and then we shot our hands up into the air like spaceships.

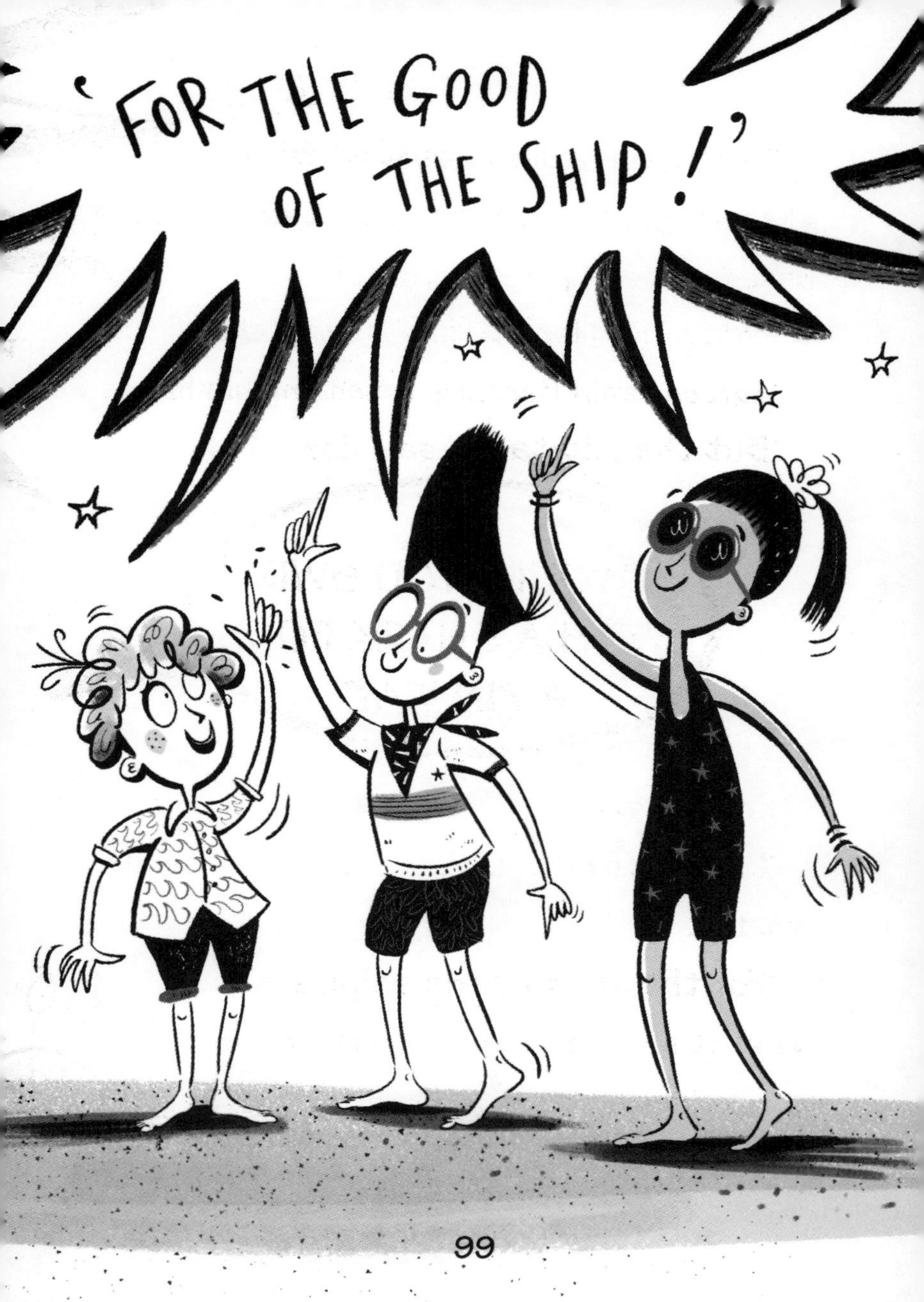
'FOR THE GOOD OF THE SHIP!'

Lucy laughed. '**You guys are so weird**,' she said. 'Come on, Butterbutt, let's go and play in the sand.'

'**Don't** let Butterbutt run away again!' I called after him.

'I don't care what you say, she's definitely <u>**NOT**</u> a beach cat!'

CHAPTER 8

QUARANTINE

In the car on the way home, Na-Na made us **PROMISE** not to tell my mum and dad that Lucy had run off.

'They'll overreact,' she said, quite rightly. 'It can be our little **secret**, right?'

We all nodded.

'Is this a good time to try to get out of weeding her garden?' Zoe whispered.

Apparently her whisper wasn't quiet enough.

'You all still have to weed my garden!' said Na-Na. **'A deal is a deal!'**

'A deal is a deal,' we chorused back.

'Good,' said Na-Na. 'To seal the deal, I'll even order **PIZZA** for dinner.'

We all cheered. Then Zoe whispered again, this time more quietly. 'But there won't be any **squid on** it, right?'

'I heard that!' said Na-Na. 'Who puts squid on pizza? We're getting pepperoni and pineapple.'

'Na-Na hears **everything**,' I whispered as quietly as I possibly could.

'He's right, I do!' said Na-Na. **'I'm always listening.'**

'Your grandma is pretty **COOL**,' said Zoe.

I nodded. 'Yeah, I know.'

Back at my house, after we'd weeded the garden and had our promised pizza for dinner, we went up to my room to strategize.

'Sam,' said Bernard, 'I've been thinking.'

'Of course you have,' I said. 'You're **always** thinking.'

'I know we can't go to the party because it is too scary—'

'Too **DANGEROUS**,' I interrupted. 'Not too scary. I'm **<u>NOT</u>** scared.'

'Right, too dangerous. But . . .'

'But what?'

'But how are we supposed to go back to school if we aren't going to the party?' said Bernard. 'Everyone will make **fun of us!**'

'He's right,' said Zoe. 'Nobody will ever invite us to **birthday parties** again!'

They had a point.

'I don't believe it has come down to this,' I said, shaking my head. 'Get eaten by **actual sharks**, or get eaten by the sharks of the playground.'

'There are sharks **in the playground?**' said Zoe.

'It's a metaphor,' I explained. I'd recently learned about metaphors on SPACE BLASTERS.

A metaphor

'It means that Ralph and his friends are like **sharks**, but not real ones.'

Bernard nodded. 'A shark could **NEVER** actually exist in the playground,' he said.

'Can we get back to the actual problem?' said Zoe.

'We definitely **can't go** to the party,' I said. 'We'll think of something.'

'Sam, what would the SPACE BLASTERS do?' said Bernard.

This was a big moment. My friends never usually ask me what the SPACE BLASTERS would do. I just tell them about the SPACE BLASTERS without them asking.

I thought hard. 'Well, once, when there was an **intergalactic plague**, they went into quarantine.'

'What's **QUARANTINE?**' said Zoe.

'It's when you have to lock yourself up in a small space for the greater good, or because the outside world is too **dangerous**.'

DANGER KEEP OUT

'Can you **EVER** go back outside?'

'Once the danger has passed – in our case, after the birthday party,' I said.

'That sounds . . . pretty **extreme**,' said Zoe.

'I think it's our only option,' I said. 'Since we're already at my house, we should probably quarantine ourselves in my room. Tonight.'

Zoe looked at Bernard. 'What do you think?' she said.

Bernard nodded. 'Sam's right. It is our **only** logical option.'

Zoe frowned. 'I don't know,' she said. 'It doesn't sound that logical to me . . .'

'If it's good enough for the **SPACE BLASTERS**, it's good enough for us,' I said. 'Now come on — we've got to sneak down to the kitchen to get **supplies!** We're going to be here for a while, so we'd better stock up.'

CHAPTER 9

PRAWN CRACKERS AND PYJAMAS

We **sneaked down** into the kitchen and grabbed all of our favourite snacks. Or at least, all of my favourite snacks.

'Do you have **goldfish crackers?**' asked Bernard.

I shook my head. 'We've got prawn crackers!' I said.

'Prawn crackers sound **WEIRD**,' said Bernard dubiously.

'How do they sound weirder than goldfish crackers?' I said.

Bernard nodded and took the bag of prawn crackers. **'Good point.'**

'Zoe, what do you want?' I asked.

'Do you have cookies?'

'Of course,' I said. My family don't have all the normal snacks but we always have cookies. 'Oreos?'

'PERFECT!'

I grabbed some apples and carrots because I knew in order to survive we'd need nutrients. On **SPACE BLASTERS** they had **special** nutrient packs, but we'd have to manage with what we had.

'This . . . is what we are going to live on?' said Zoe, eying everything we'd gathered.

'What else do you want?' I said.

Her eyes lit up. 'Let's get the **leftover pizza!**'

So we also grabbed the pizza box. And a big bottle of **lemonade**.

Back up in my room, we put **EVERYTHING** on the floor.

'Well, we've got enough food to last us a while,' I said.

'But what are we going to do?' said Zoe.

'What do you mean?'

'Won't we get **bored?** Maybe we should get your TV.'

I looked around my room. I didn't think it was boring. **It had everything I needed!** My books and magazines and toys and even Fang!

'Fang!' I said suddenly.

'What about Fang?' said Bernard.

'What is Fang going to eat?'

'What does he usually eat?'

'LIVE MICE.'

Zoe frowned. 'Where does he get them?'

'We get them from **the pet store**,' I said. 'I have to feed him once a week.' At first, I was a little nervous about feeding Fang, but now I'm used to it. All part of **being brave**.

'Well, maybe we can get him out and he can find his own mice,' said Zoe.

'But what if he can't find mice and then he eats us?' said Bernard.

'He **WON'T** eat us,' I said with as much authority as I could muster.

'Are you sure about that?' said Zoe.

'Yeah, *how* sure are you?' said Bernard.

I went over to **Fang's cage** and looked him right in the eye. 'You won't eat us, right, Fang?' He looked back at me. We had a staring contest for a while.

He won – he **ALWAYS DOES**. Then he stuck his tongue out at me. He always does that too.

'I'm **pretty sure** he won't eat us,' I said, turning back to my friends.

'But how do you know?' wailed Bernard. 'I need **PROOF!**'

'We just spoke in our **secret** language,' I said.

'What secret language?' said Zoe as she opened the pack of **Oreos.**

'I can't tell you because then it wouldn't be a secret!' I said. 'And stop eating the Oreos — we need those to last a **whole week!**'

'Sam,' said Bernard in an urgent whisper, 'what if we need to go to the **BATHROOM?**'

'Hmm . . .' I said. I hadn't thought about that.

'And what am I going to tell my mum?' said Zoe.

'Calm down! Calm down! We'll figure it out,' I said. This wasn't going well **AT ALL**.

'You don't sound very calm,' said Bernard.

My door opened. 'Are you guys playing a game? Can I play?' It was Lucy. And Butterbutt.

'Lucy! **Close the door!** We're in quarantine!'

Lucy ignored me of course, and put down Butterbutt, who promptly raced over to **Fang's tank**. 'And watch Butterbutt! Make sure she doesn't open Fang's tank again!'

Butterbutt pawed at the tank. Fang hid behind a rock.

'Lucy! **Get out of here** and take Butterbutt with you!' I said.

'Sam!' Now my mum was at the door! Doesn't **anybody** know what quarantine means? 'Be nice to your sister.' She frowned at all the food on my floor. 'And you know you aren't allowed to eat in your room.'

'**WE'RE IN QUARANTINE!**' I yelled. I really need a lock on my door. '**CAN EVERYBODY PLEASE LEAVE?**'

My mum raised her eyebrows.

'**WU GABO!**[11], why are you in quarantine? Is this a SPACE BLASTERS' thing?'

I couldn't think of an answer. I looked over at Zoe and Bernard and telepathically asked them to help me out. Zoe nodded, and I knew

---

[11] Wu Gabo is my full Chinese name. My mum always calls me by my Chinese name when she thinks I'm up to no good.

she had received my **telepathic message**.

'It's just a game, Mrs Wu,' she said. 'Nothing to worry about!'

'**Okay . . .**' said my mum, looking unconvinced. 'But Sam still isn't allowed to have food in his room . . .'

'Just this once? **Please?**' I asked.

'Yeah, please, Mrs Wu? **Please?**' added Bernard.

My mum sighed. 'Fine. I'm not going to be the mean mum today. I'm too tired.'

'**HOORAY!**' we all shouted.

'Thanks, Mum!' I said.

'Thanks, Mrs Wu!' said Zoe.

'Oh and, Mum?' I said.

She turned back. '**Yes, Sam?**'

'Can you bring the TV up into my room? Since we're in quarantine?'

My mum **scowled**. 'No, Sam. You can't have the TV in your room.' She looked at Zoe and Bernard. 'And your parents will be here soon.'

Soon! We were going to have to figure out a way to barricade ourselves in my room.

'Sam, **can I use the bathroom** now?' said Bernard.

'Fine,' I said. Nobody was respecting the

quarantine. 'But be **quick!**'

'Sam, I don't really want to sleep in the **same room as Fang**,' said Zoe. 'I don't know if this is a good idea.'

'Fang is an **EXCELLENT** roommate,' I said. 'He doesn't snore or anything.'

'But what if he gets out again? You know I like Fang, but I don't want to wake up with him on my **PILLOW!**'

I sighed and sat down in the middle of **all our snacks**. 'This plan is never going to work, is it?'

'You guys are **boring**,' said Lucy. 'I'm going to play in my room.'

'Take Butterbutt with you!' I said.

Bernard came back into my room. 'Sam, I've been thinking. I don't have **ANY** pyjamas, and I don't think I'll fit into yours,' he said, sitting down on the bag of prawn crackers. They crunched **loudly** under him. **'Whoops**,' he said. 'Can we get some more of these? **Prawn crackers** are pretty good.'

'Are pyjamas and prawn crackers all you can think about?' I yelled. 'This is **SERIOUS** business!'

'How long do we have to stay in here again?' asked Zoe.

'Just until the party is finished,' I said. This was getting exhausting.

'That is a **WHOLE WEEK** away!'

'I know,' I said. I was starting to seriously doubt this plan.

'Zoe! **Your dad is here!**' my mum shouted up the stairs.

'**QUICK!** Close my door!' I said. 'We have to block it!'

'But, Sam, I want to sleep in my own bed,' said Zoe.

'Me too,' said Bernard.

'But **what are we going to do** about Ralph and Regina's party?' I said.

Zoe looked at me. 'I'm sorry, Sam. I think we're going to have to go to the party. But we can go without getting in the water.'

'But what if something happens and we **HAVE** to get in the water?' I said. 'We have to be prepared for **the unexpected!**' I learned that from Spaceman Jack.

'**I can't get in the water!**' said Bernard, sounding panicked. 'I can't swim!'

'Hmmm,' I said. 'That **IS** a problem. Because then the shark will **DEFINITELY** get you.'

'I have **an idea!**' said Zoe, standing up and pointing in the air.

Bernard and I looked at her.

'Bernard, you are going to learn how to swim,' she said.

It was **so obvious!** Why hadn't I thought of that?

'But that doesn't fix our **shark problem**,' I said.

Zoe crouched down and put her face close to mine. 'Sam, did we or didn't we defeat the Ghost King?'

'**WE DID!**' I said.

'We did?' said Bernard. 'I thought it wasn't really the Ghost King . . .'

'SHH! Listen to Zoe!' I said. I could tell she was about to say something GENIUS. It was as if she was Captain Jane and I was Spaceman Jack and Bernard was . . . well, Bernard was like Five-Eyed Frank, their alien best friend. I bet **Five-Eyed Frank** doesn't know how to swim either.

'If we can defeat the **Ghost King**, we can defeat a shark! Are you with me?' said Zoe.

'**We can!**' I said, standing up too. 'Even if it is the Evil Shark Lord! Or his cousin Crazy Charlie! We are the SPACE BLASTERS and we can do anything!'

'But how am I going to learn to **SWIM?**' said Bernard. 'That is our **biggest** problem!'

'Well, **technically** that is your biggest problem,' I said.

'Sam!' said Zoe.

'Sorry,' I said. **'Don't worry**, Bernard, we'll think of something.'

'I've already thought of something,' said Zoe proudly. Really, she's **just** like Captain Jane!

'Tomorrow we're **going to the pool**,' she said.

'And then what?' said Bernard.

'My sister is on the swimming team. She can teach you how to swim!'

'Your **SISTER?**' said Bernard. 'But she's . . . she's . . .'

'She's in **HIGH SCHOOL**,' I said. High school is like another world! It was as if Zoe had said a **Ziggy-monster**[12] could teach Bernard to swim.

---

[12] Ziggy-monsters are VERY dangerous water monsters that live on water planets in the Space Blasters' universe.

'I'll ask her,' said Zoe. 'Mallory's nice. Sort of. If she's in a good mood.'

'What if she's not in a **GOOD** mood? Am I going to **drown?**' said Bernard.

'We'll find out!' I said. Just then my mum opened the door.

'Come on, Zoe,' she said. 'Your dad is waiting.'

'**Bye, guys,**' said Zoe. 'I'll see you tomorrow!' She ran through the door after my mum.

'This is a **horrible** plan,' moaned Bernard.

'A horrible plan is better than no plan,' I said. I learned that from SPACE BLASTERS.

CHAPTER 10

UNDERWATER SPACESUIT

'I am <u>**NOT**</u> wearing the armbands **like a baby**,' said Bernard, stomping his foot.

'Bernard, you have to wear them!' said Zoe. 'It's the **rule**.'

It was the next day and we were at the outdoor pool. **The sun was hot**, the pool was wet. Everything was going to plan. Except Bernard.

'But everyone will **laugh** at me!' said Bernard.

'We won't,' I said. '**I promise**.' Because that is what good friends do. They don't laugh at their friends even when they look **a little bit silly**. Like he didn't laugh at me when I had my **INCIDENT** at the Space Museum.

'Ralph probably would laugh at you,' said Zoe, 'but he's not here.'

'Okay, **FINE**,' said Bernard, pulling the armbands on. 'I feel **ridiculous**.'

'You look ridiculous,' I said cheerfully. 'But think of it like your underwater **spacesuit!**'

'I thought the reason for these was to make sure I **DIDN'T** go underwater!' said Bernard.

As usual, **Bernard made a good point**.

Just then, Zoe's sister Mallory walked up.

She was wearing **big red sunglasses** and had a whistle around her neck. 'Are you ready to go?' she said. 'I've got **lifeguard duty** later, so if we are going to do this, we've got to do it now.'

Bernard gulped. 'Right now?'

'Right now,' said Mallory. Then she smiled. **'You'll be fine**. I bet you'll even have fun. And if you don't, I'll take you guys for ice cream after.'

'**WHOA, WHOA**,' I said. Now that ice cream was involved, the stakes were raised. 'What if he **DOES** have fun? Do we still get ice cream?'

Mallory rolled her eyes. 'We'll see. But nobody is getting any **ice cream** unless this kid gets in the pool, **pronto**.'

'Come on, Bernard!' I said. I really wanted some ice cream. As I said, it was a hot day.

He still looked nervous.

I knew what would help. I leaned towards him and whispered the **SPACE BLASTERS'** motto: 'Do it for the universe.'

Bernard took a deep breath. **'For the universe!'** he shouted.

But then he just stood there, staring at me. His eyes looked **HUGE** behind his swimming goggles.

'For the universe!' I said again. 'You can do it!' I went over and poked him in the side because he was as still as a **statue**. 'Bernard? You okay?' I said.

'I just need a minute,' he said. And then

he took another deep breath.

'For the universe!'

he roared.

And then, before I realized what he was doing, he ran towards the pool and jumped in!

'Well, that's one way to start a swimming

lesson,' said Mallory, walking to the side of the pool and watching Bernard flounder.

'**MALLORY! GO AND SAVE BERNARD!**' Zoe yelled. '**ARE YOU A LIFEGUARD OR WHAT?**'

'He's fine,' said Mallory. 'Look.'

And it was true! Bernard had popped right back up because of the armbands.

'These are great!' he said, gesturing at his armbands. 'It's as if **I'M FLYING!**'

'I told you they were like your spacesuit!' I said, giving him a thumbs up.

'Okay, you guys, I'm going to show Mr **Underwater Spacesuit** how to actually swim, so why don't you go and play over there? I don't want you watching and making him nervous.'

We nodded.

'**Hey, Mallory?**' said Zoe.

'Yeah, Z?'

'Thanks.'

Mallory smiled and tugged on Zoe's ponytail.

'Does this mean we get **ice cream?**' I asked.

'Get out of here,' Mallory said, but she was still smiling. So I thought our chances of getting ice cream were pretty good.

CHAPTER 11

AN ATTACK IN THE POOL!

While Mallory taught Bernard some swimming basics — '**Kick your legs!** No, not like that, like this! Keep your head up!' — Zoe and I got in the **other side** of the shallow end of the pool.

I'm a pretty good swimmer, but not the best. Zoe is an **EXCELLENT** swimmer. She can do all the strokes and even knows how to dive. I mostly just doggy-paddle.

'I'm going to jump off the **diving board**,' she said, pointing at it.

It was **SO HIGH** up in the air that I had thought it was a plane flying overhead. '**Want to come?**'

I squinted upwards. 'You know what,' I said, 'I think it is **best** if we stay in the water.'

Zoe frowned. 'Why? **I LOVE the diving board!**'

'Because we should stay nearby in case Bernard needs us,' I said. 'Part of being a **team**.'

'But my sister is with Bernard,' said Zoe. 'He'll be fine.'

'It's all about moral support,' I said. And then I lowered my voice. 'Besides, what if the **Evil Shark Lord** gets in the pool and we have to save Bernard?'

'What?' shrieked Zoe. 'The Evil Shark Lord isn't going to get in the pool.'

I pointed at a dark, shadowy corner of the pool.

The **darkest** part of the deep end.

'How can you be so sure? Do we really

know what is in the **deep end?**' I said.

'Sam! **Sharks don't swim in pools**,' scoffed Zoe. 'Even I know that.'

'Zoe, don't you remember when Fang got in the **pipes** in my house?'

'Of course I remember!'

'Well, if snakes can get in pipes, then surely sharks can get in pools,' I said. I wished Bernard was with us. He'd see the logic in my thoughts. He always does.

'There isn't a **shark in the pool!**' said Zoe, splashing me.

'Maybe not now,' I said. 'But there could be. **It's possible.**'

'I don't think so,' said Zoe.

'Well, would you swim in the deep end? In the **DARK** part of the **deep end?**'

Zoe squirmed. 'Well, when I jump off the diving board, I land in the deep end.'

'But not the **REAL** deep end,' I said, pointing again at the far, dark corner of the pool where **nobody** ever goes. It's where pool toys inevitably end up, but once they get sucked over there, we **never** get them back. 'And you want to know why?' I went on.

Zoe sighed. 'Tell me why,' she said.

'Because you **KNOW** that there might be a shark there,' I said smugly.

Just then, I felt a sharp **BITE** on my leg!

'Argh!

IT'S THE SHARK! IT CAME IN THE SHALLOW END!'

I flailed in the pool, splashing **everywhere**, water going in my nose and in my eyes.

'Calm down – it's just my brother Toby,' said Zoe.

Toby popped up in the water next to me, grinning.

'**Gotcha!**' he said, pinching his fingers together like crab claws. Then he laughed. 'Sam! You yelled so **loud!**'

'I did not,' I said. 'I was . . . laughing. I'm very ticklish.'

Toby giggled and pinched me again.

'**OW!**' I said.

'Toby! Stop that,' said Zoe.

But Toby just kept laughing. 'Pinch, pinch!' he said.

I was so relieved that it wasn't an **actual shark**, I didn't even mind.

We played in the pool with Toby until Bernard finished his swimming lesson with Mallory. I couldn't believe it when he actually **swam** over to us![13]

---

[13] He still had his armbands on, so technically it was more of a float-swim – but I was still impressed.

'Bernard!' I said. 'You're a natural!'

'**I know!**' he said. 'Look at me kick!'

Zoe and I watched Bernard kick for a few seconds and applauded when he was done.

'So . . . when do you take the armbands off?' said Zoe.

Bernard looked horrified. '**Take them OFF?**'

'Well, yeah – you are going to take them off, right?'

'Not if I **don't have to!** Why would I take them off? Look what I can do in them!' He **rolled over** on to his back and floated.

'Easy-peasy!' he said.

'I can do that too,' said Zoe.
'**Without** armbands.' And then she floated
on her back!

'**Show-offs**,' I muttered, because I
definitely couldn't float on my back.

'Bernard was **great** today,' said Mallory.
'You guys should be really
proud of him.'

'Does this mean we get ice cream?' I said.

'You get ice cream,' said Mallory.

'**YAY!**' said Zoe, turning and doing a somersault underwater.

'Cool!' said Bernard. Then he looked at Mallory. 'Can you teach **me** how to do that next time?'

Mallory laughed. 'Look at you wanting to learn how to do things underwater. You'll be a **champion swimmer** in no time.'

'When you say "no time",' I said, tapping her on the shoulder, 'how much **time** do you actually mean? Because we need Bernard to be able to swim by Saturday.'

'He still needs a few more lessons,' said Mallory. 'But we'll see where he is by the end of the week. And worst case, he can always wear his **armbands** . . .'

'You mean my **UNDERWATER SPACESUIT**,' interrupted Bernard.

'Exactly. You'll have your Underwater Spacesuit if you need it,' she said. 'Now come on, let's go and get **ice cream**. You've earned it.'

CHAPTER 12

YOU CAN'T GET CHICKEN POX TWICE

The next day at school, we met at our usual spot by the fence.

'Since Bernard can **nearly swim** now, we can go to the party!' said Zoe. 'I'm **SO** excited!'

'Hmm . . .' I said.

'What's wrong?' said Zoe.

'Nothing is wrong . . . but I've been thinking,' I said, **walking in a circle**. Spaceman Jack always walks in **a circle**

when he is trying to solve a problem. 'I'm not
so sure we should go.'

'But **why?**' said Zoe. 'Remember the
piñata! And the cake!'

'And the **SHARKS!**'
I said, my voice squeaking
just a tiny bit.

'You said we could **outswim** the sharks,' said Bernard, munching on a carrot stick. 'That was why I learned to swim.'

'You **did say** that,' said Zoe, frowning at me.

'Well, I might have been wrong,' I admitted. 'Seriously, **THINK** about it. Zoe could probably outswim a shark because she's **so fast**—'

'Thanks, Sam,' said Zoe.

'But Bernard and I have no chance! No offence, Bernard.'

'So what are you saying?' said Zoe.

'We need to think of another reason why we can't go to the party. It is just too **dangerous!**'

Zoe sighed. 'Fine,' she said. 'If you really, really don't want to go, we won't go. But we need a good reason.'

'Of course I **want** to go,' I said. 'But we just can't!'

'Well, what are we going to tell everyone?' said Zoe.

'We could say we have **chicken pox?**' said Bernard.

'Hmm. Not a bad thought,' I said.

'We could even draw chicken pox spots on

OURSELVES!' said Bernard, getting more into the idea.

'I've already had chicken pox,' said Zoe. 'And I got it from Regina, so she'll know I'm not telling the **truth**.'

'Well, maybe you got it again!' said Bernard.

'**Everyone** knows you only get chicken pox once,' said Zoe. 'You should know that, Bernard. You're supposed to know **EVERYTHING!**'

Bernard glowered. 'I'm not a chicken pox expert,' he said. 'And I still think it is a good plan.'

'Zoe's got a point,' I said. 'And besides, my mum would be **furious** if I drew chicken pox all over myself. Remember how mad she got when we drew **tattoos on** each other?'

'We didn't know it was permanent marker!' said Zoe.

'Mine didn't come off for **weeks!**' said Bernard. Then he rolled up his sleeve and looked at his arm, as if his tattoo might still be there.

'Anyway,' I said, 'fake chicken pox isn't an option. But it was a good idea.' **Captain Jane** always listens to all of the crew's ideas, no matter how bad they might be. So I tried to do that too. 'Any other thoughts?' I asked.

Just then, Ralph came sauntering over. Wearing his bow tie, as usual.

'I heard you **babies** were too scared to come to our party,' he said with a snort. 'You weren't even really invited, so **I don't care**.'

'What do you mean we weren't invited? I have the invitation right here!' said Bernard, whipping out the invite from his pocket.

'Yeah!' I said. 'We're **DEFINITELY** invited

to your party.'

'Of **course** you are,' said a softer voice. It was Regina. She'd walked up behind us without me noticing. 'We want **you three** to come. You'll make it more fun!' She smiled at us, and even though I was mad at Ralph, I smiled back at her. So did Bernard and Zoe.

'Thanks,' said Zoe.

'I wouldn't have invited you, but Regina said we had to,' said Ralph. 'Ugh. She's so **nice** like that.'

'I invited them because I wanted to,' said Regina, elbowing Ralph in the side. 'Don't you remember that they caught a **GHOST?** I want ghost-hunters at our party!'

'Yep, we definitely **one hundred per cent** caught a ghost,' I said.

'**Sort of**,' said Bernard. I stepped in front of him.

'Anyway! If there are any ghosts at your party, **we'll** take care of them,' I went on.

Regina clapped. 'I **knew** you would!'

'There won't be ghosts at our party,' said Ralph, and then he paused. 'But there will be **SHARKS**. So I bet you won't come,' he said, smirking at us. 'I saw how scared you were of that shark at the aquarium.'

'Ralph, there aren't going to be sharks at **our birthday**,' said Regina. She smiled at me again. 'He's just joking.'

'Did you know that I've swum with sharks before?' said Ralph. 'Last summer in Hawaii. It was **AWESOME**. They can smell fear and they couldn't smell it on me.'

I have to admit, I was impressed.

'You went swimming with **SHARKS?**' I said.

'Whoa,' said Bernard.

Zoe frowned. 'I don't believe you,' she said.

'**I did!** Just ask Regina.'

We all looked over at Regina. She tugged on a loose strand of hair.

'Ralph,' she said. 'You know it wasn't sharks.'

'**IT WAS TOO!**' he said.

'What was it really?' Zoe asked.

'We swam with **dolphins**,' Regina said. 'I felt like a mermaid!'

'Wow!' said Zoe.

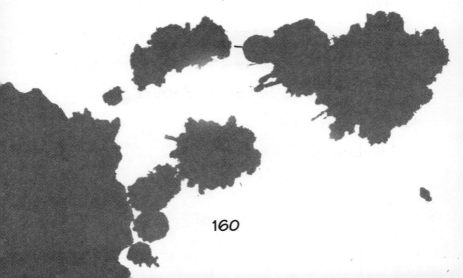

'They were **DEFINITELY** sharks,' said Ralph, scowling.

I was starting to think that maybe, just maybe, Ralph and I had more in common than I had thought. But I definitely couldn't let him be **braver than me**. Sharks or no sharks, it looked as if we were going to have to go to that party.

'If you can swim with sharks—' I started.

'**DOLPHINS**,' Zoe and Regina said at the same time.

'**We** can swim with sharks,' I finished, gesturing around at me, Bernard and Zoe.

'Sam, I can barely swim **at all!**' Bernard whispered. 'And you just said it was too dangerous to go!'

I ignored him.

'We're **definitely** going to your birthday party!' I said.

'We are?' said Bernard.

'Well, if you really do come—' said Ralph.

'Oh, **WE'RE COMING!**' I said. There was no turning back now. Spaceman Jack always says that once you commit to a plan, you have to see it through.

'You'd better bring me a **really good** present,' said Ralph.

'Of course,' I said, because that's **birthday party law**. You have to bring someone a present to their birthday party. Even if that person is Ralph. I looked over at Regina. 'We'll bring you presents too,' I said.

She beamed. 'I'm just happy you guys are coming to our party.'

After **Ralph and Regina** walked away, Bernard turned to me with wide eyes.

'Sam,' he said. 'Are we **REALLY** going to the party?'

'We'd better be,' said Zoe. 'I'm sick of all this going back and forth.'

'But what about the **sharks?**' Bernard wailed. 'What are we going to do?'

'I've got a **plan**,' I said.

Bernard **groaned**. 'Not another plan!'

'You'll like this one,' I said. 'It starts with us going to the library!'

CHAPTER 13

THE EIGHT SENSES OF DOOM!

So after school that day, we went to the library.

Bernard was **THRILLED**. The library is his favourite place. He loves to look up facts. And this was just what we needed.

'Okay,' I said when we were inside. 'First things first . . .'

'**Shh!**' someone behind me said. 'This is a library!'

I turned around. It was **a girl** a few years

165

older than us. 'I **know** it is a library,' I said.

'Then **BE QUIET!**' she hissed back at me. 'I'm trying to do my homework!'

I've heard that when you get older you get more homework. Maybe that's why she was so **grumpy**.

'Someone should invent a loud library,' I said. 'It is very hard to keep quiet when you are discovering **EXCITING** things!'

'Discover exciting things more quietly,' grumpy homework girl said.

'**Come on**,' said Bernard. 'Let's go to the science section!'

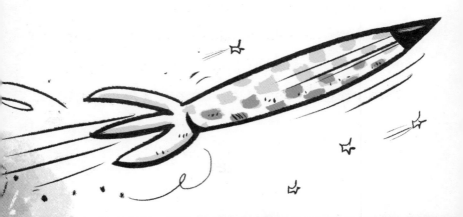

The science section was **HUGE** – so huge that the shelves went all the way to the ceiling!

'Um, Bernard,' I said, tipping my head back so I could see the tops of the shelves. 'How do we even reach those books?'

'How do we even **READ** them? They look like **ENCYCLOPEDIAS!**' said Zoe.

Bernard beamed. 'They **ARE** encyclopedias! And watch this!'

He jogged around the corner (this shows just how excited he was – Bernard never jogs unless he absolutely has to) and came back lugging a ladder on wheels.

'**Ta-da!**' he said, looking proud of himself.

'That doesn't look very safe,' I said, eying it warily. <u>NOT </u>that I am afraid of heights, because I'm not afraid of **anything**, but you know – safety first.

'It's **fine!** I've seen the librarians go up it loads of times!' said Bernard. 'Just **HOLD IT STILL** for me.'

'Maybe we should both hold it still,' I said. 'We don't want it to roll away!'

Bernard wheeled the ladder over to the S section. '**I see the books!**' he said, pointing far, far up. 'I'll get them.'

'Have you ever seen anyone go up that **high?**' I asked.

He shook his head. 'No, but I can do it,' he said. He looked a little **nervous**.

'Are you sure?' said Zoe. 'I can go if you

want.' Zoe is used to heights from jumping off the diving board.

Bernard nodded. '**I'm sure**,' he said. 'If I can learn to swim, I can climb this ladder.' Then he looked at both of us. 'Just hold it really steady and let me know if someone comes — I think only librarians are allowed to go up it.'

'Maybe we should just get a librarian?' said Zoe.

'Bernard can do it!' I said. 'This is his **MOMENT!**' I was very proud of Bernard. I lowered my voice and raised my hand in our signature **SPACE BLASTERS** salute.

'For the universe!' I whispered.

'**For the universe!**' Zoe and Bernard whispered back.

And then Bernard was **up the ladder!**

'**Whoa**, it's pretty high up here!' he said.

'Don't look down!' I said.

'You aren't **that** high,' said Zoe. 'But hurry up — I think someone is coming!'

'Give me a second,' said Bernard. 'I've got them!' Then he paused. 'They're **pretty heavy** . . . I don't know how I'm going to go back down the ladder with them.'

'Why don't you drop them?' said Zoe.

'**WHAT IF THEY LAND ON OUR HEADS?**' I said.

'Shh!' said Zoe. 'Bernard, just be careful with your aim.'

'**BERNARD HAS TERRIBLE AIM!**' I said in a whisper-shout. A whisper-shout is when you want to shout but you have to be **quiet**.

'DON'T YOU REMEMBER THE BASKETBALL SITUATION?'

'We don't talk about that!' Bernard whisper-shouted back down. 'I've got this! Just watch out!'

Of all the shark-related **ways to die**, getting hit on the head with a book about sharks had to be the worst.

I closed my eyes tight and waited.

'One, two, three!' said Bernard. There was a rustle of pages past my ear and a

right next to me.

'**YOU ALMOST GOT ME!**' I exclaimed.

'But I didn't!' said Bernard. 'Stop shaking — it's making the ladder wobble.'

'**I'm not shaking!** And get back down here so we can start researching.'

'My idea is to learn as much about the enemy as we can, find their weaknesses and have a **PLAN OF ATTACK**,' I said. We had our shark research books and our notebooks and were sitting on a table far from any other library goers. We didn't want to get in trouble for not whispering.

'**The enemy?**' said Zoe.

'The sharks!' I told her.

'We're going to **attack sharks?**' she said. 'That sounds like the worst plan you've ever had, Sam!'

I shook my head. '**NO, NO, NO**. When I say "plan of attack", I mean we'll just be **prepared** for them. It's a saying. I learned it from Captain Jane. So, first thing is to find out everything we can about **sharks**. Bernard, what have you found?'

Bernard looked up from his book. 'I've learned quite a lot,' he said. He sounded a little nervous. 'I think they might be even **more dangerous** than we first thought.'

'How is that possible?' I sputtered. I already thought sharks were the most dangerous things in the **UNIVERSE!**

'Just **tell us the facts**, Bernard,' said Zoe. 'We're ready.'

'Well,' said Bernard, 'first of all, sharks can have over three thousand teeth . . .'

'**THREE THOUSAND?**' I said.

Bernard ignored me and kept going. 'And they have no bones and are made mostly of **muscle**.'

'So they are made of just muscles and teeth?' said Zoe. 'Like a **super villain!**'

'Exactly like a super villain,' I said. 'Like the Evil Shark Lord!'

'What else, Bernard?' said Zoe.

'They **NEVER** stop moving,' he said.

'**Oh no**,' I groaned. 'So much for my plan to only go in the water when they were sleeping.'

'And they have **EIGHT** senses,' he said. 'Here, I wrote them down.'

'**EIGHT?**' I exclaimed. 'How many do we have?'

'Five,' said Bernard. 'We've got touch, sight, hearing, taste and smell. **Sharks** have all of those plus they can sense water currents, vibrations **AND** electrical fields.'

'Electrical fields! Are they like robots?' said Zoe.

'**Actually**,' said Bernard, 'all things with a heartbeat give off an electric pulse. Sharks use their **electro-sensors** to sense your heartbeat in the water.'

'Electro-what?' said Zoe.

'I don't care what it is called,' I said with a shudder. 'What are all these senses even for?'

'Mostly for finding food,' said Bernard. '**THEY ARE THE PERFECT PREDATOR!**' I wailed. '**WE WON'T HAVE A CHANCE!**'

'Actually,' said Bernard again, 'I've been researching, and the chances of a person getting **eaten by a shark** are slim.'

'How slim?'

'*Very* slim,' said Bernard, looking me in the eye. 'You're more likely to have a vending

drinks machine
fall on you, or
get struck by
lightning,
or for a
coconut
to fall on your head!'

'Thanks, Bernard.
Now I'm just going to be
worried about **ALL** of
those things,' I moaned.
'And we still don't have a
plan for the shark.'

'Well,' said Bernard, 'we could
always try what the Aztecs did.'

'Who are the **Aztecs?**' said Zoe.

'Don't you remember my presentation on them last year?' said Bernard.

'You do a lot of presentations,' I said.

'The Aztecs were a tribe that lived in Central America **HUNDREDS AND HUNDREDS** of years ago and they were **super smart!** They built temples and were the **inventors** of chocolate.'

'I mean, I **love** chocolate, but chocolate won't save us from sharks!' I said. 'Tell me what the Aztecs did about sharks.'

'Well, they used to attach **chilli peppers** to their canoes to keep the sharks away.'

I frowned. 'Like pickle juice keeps ghosts away?'

'**EXACTLY**,' said Bernard. 'So we'll bring chilli peppers to the party!'

'Where are we going to get **chilli peppers?**' asked Zoe.

I grinned. I knew where. 'Don't you remember what Na-Na is growing in her garden?'

CHAPTER 14

A PARTY . . . FOR SHARKS!

Then it was time.

Time for Ralph and Regina's **beach birthday bash**.

Or 'shark attack take two', as I was calling it in my head.

But we were ready. Or as ready as we were going to be. After the library, we'd sneaked into Na-Na's garden and **stolen** some of her chillies. Actually, we **TRIED** to sneak into her garden, but she is always watching, so she caught us. It was really **pretty lucky** she caught us, because she told us that chillies could

No wonder sharks are afraid of them!

BURN YOUR EYES OUT

and made us wear gloves before we touched them. And then she helped us tie them on to string for us to wear around our waists. We told her it was for an **art project**. If you ever need to trick an adult, say it is for a school project. Works every time.

We all had our **shark-repelling chilli-**

pepper belts, Bernard had his armbands and Zoe had her big sunglasses. The sunglasses didn't have anything to do with the plan, but she **insisted** on wearing them.

Lucy tried to come to the party but I told her it was for **big kids** only. I felt a little bad about that so I promised her I'd go back to the beach with her next weekend but **ONLY** if she didn't bring Butterbutt.

I also checked my backpack before leaving, just to make sure Butterbutt hadn't sneaked in. He's kind of a **ninja cat** – you never know what he'll get up to.

By the time we arrived at the beach, our **whole** class was at the party! There were balloons everywhere, a shark cake the size of a real shark and, just like Zoe promised, **A MAGICIAN**. He was making balloon animals. Everyone wanted a shark. **Not me** — I didn't need any more sharks in my life. I asked for a giraffe.

'Look who came to the party — **Scaredy-Cat Sam!**' said Ralph with a sneer.

'Happy birthday, Ralph,' I said, holding out his present. Because even if he was Ralph, it was still his birthday. 'Thank you for inviting me to your birthday.' My mum always makes me say **THANK YOU**.

'I told you, I didn't invite you — Regina did,' he said. But he still took his present.

'Well, tell Regina thank you,' I said.

'**Tell her yourself**,' said Ralph. 'She's right here.' Regina had just walked up to us.

'Happy birthday, Regina,' I said, handing her a present.

'Thank you, Sam!' she said, smiling at me.

Ralph was staring at my **shark-repellent** belt. 'What **IS** that?'

'None of your business,' I said quickly.

'I think it looks **nice**,' said Regina. 'Zoe and Bernard are wearing them too.'

'**Losers**,' said Ralph. Then he smiled, but it wasn't a nice smile, it was a **shark smile**. 'Bet you are too scared to go in the water,' he said.

'AM NOT,'

I said.

'ARE TOO,'

he said.

'AM NOT,'

I said.

'**Prove it**,' said Ralph.

'You don't have to prove anything, Sam,'
said Regina.

I took a **deep breath** and looked out at
the sea. This was it. This was the moment
to prove once and for all that I wasn't
Scaredy-Cat Sam.

And then I saw it.

I SAW THE SHARK!

But I didn't *only* see the shark. There was a

man – an old man – right next to the shark!

'There's an old man about to get attacked by a shark!' I said, pointing.

'**WHAT?**' yelled Ralph, looking at the sea. 'Where?'

'I'll get help!' cried Regina, running back up the beach towards the **lifeguard** stand.

I did what I had to do. **I ran**.

Not away, like I usually do.

But towards the sea. Just like Spaceman Jack would.

As he says, **sometimes we have to run into danger to be a hero**.

I ran as fast as I could, my chilli-pepper belt **flapping in the wind**. I was kicking up sand and running through sandcastles but I couldn't stop. I didn't want to be too late!

I ran into the water, the waves around me, and went straight for the old man. He was **even older** than Na-Na! If Na-Na is ever in the sea all by herself and about to get eaten by a shark, I hope someone will save her too.

'Hey, you!' I yelled. 'Get out! There's a

SHARK

behind you!'

CHAPTER 15

CAKE FOR HEROES

I was **frozen** in fear. I couldn't move. The
waves were getting **higher** (almost to my
knees) and the shark was getting **closer**
and the man **STILL** wasn't getting out of
the water and I closed my eyes and hoped
Bernard was right about the chilli-pepper
belt repelling **sharks**, and then . . .

'**That's not a shark**,' said the old man, who had finally swum over and was standing next to me. 'That's a dolphin.'

I opened my eyes and blinked. **A DOLPHIN?** I squinted into the sun and saw the fin heading back out into the open sea. Now that **I was closer**, I could tell that it didn't really look like a shark fin. I wondered if the '**shark**' we'd seen with Butterbutt had been the same

dolphin! Or maybe it was its friend.

'It's **good luck** to see a dolphin,' said the old man, smiling at me. 'Did you come in here thinking it was a shark? Why would you do a thing like that?'

'I didn't want you to get **eaten**,' I said.

The old man shook his head. He was wearing a wet suit and looked as if he could have been a member of the SPACE BLASTERS. A really old member though.

'Young man, that was a **<u>VERY</u> brave** thing for you to do,' he said. 'Thank you.'

'But you were never in any **actual danger**,' I said.

'You didn't know that. You are a **HERO!**'

SAM IS
A
HERO

I grinned. I'd never been called a **hero** before. I knew Spaceman Jack would be proud.

'Why don't we go have some cake to celebrate?' he said.

'Cake?' I said. How did he know there was **cake on the beach?**

'Yes! It's my granddaughter and grandson's birthday today.'

'You're Ralph and Regina's **grandpa?**' I said. I couldn't **believe** it!

'Oh, do you know Ralphie and Regina? Wonderful! Well, let's go and join them.'

RALPHIE? I couldn't imagine anyone calling Ralph 'Ralphie'! I smiled to myself.

I went back up to the party with Ralph and Regina's grandpa. The lifeguard had come by the party because Regina had told him there was a shark. But the lifeguard could tell with his **binoculars** that it was a dolphin.

'**There was <u>NO</u> shark**,' said Ralph with a sneer.

Then he saw who was next to me.

'Grandpa!' he said. 'Where'd you go?'

'Oh, I just went for a little dip. And this **brave young man** thought he saw a shark about to get me, so he ran to save me. You're **lucky** to have him as a friend.'

'He's not my friend,' said Ralph, glaring at me. 'And I still think he's a **scaredy-cat**.'

'He's my friend,' said Regina with a big smile. 'Thank you for saving my grandpa!'

'**You're welcome**,' I said.

Zoe and Bernard ran up to us. Bernard had cake on his face.

'Sam! Sam! We just heard you saved someone from **a shark!** What happened?' he said.

'Let me get some cake too, and then I'll tell you the **WHOLE STORY**,' I said.

The shark-shaped cake was delicious. The magician was great. The piñata was full of sweets. And everyone wanted to hear about my brave **adventure**.

'I would have gone in too,' said Ralph.

And, because it was his **birthday**, I didn't argue with him. I just nodded and said, 'I know, **I just got there first**.'

'Sam,' said Regina, who was sitting next

to me, eating another piece of cake, 'now that you've chased a ghost **AND** saved my grandpa from a shark, do you think you could come over sometime and get the **zombie werewolf** in our basement?'

Ralph's eyes got **HUGE**. 'Regina! We don't talk about the **zombie werewolf!**'

I looked at Zoe and Bernard, who were both frantically shaking their heads and mouthing, '**NO, NO, NO**,' at me.

'Of course I can check out the zombie werewolf,' I said in my **bravest** voice. 'I'll bring Zoe and Bernard with me.'

Totally <u>NOT</u> terrifying!

Zoe and Bernard groaned.
'Oh no,' said Bernard.
I grinned at them. '**For the universe!**' I said, **shooting**

my hand towards the sky. *Zoe and Bernard are my team, I thought, just like Captain Jane, Spaceman Jack and Five-Eyed Frank are a team on* SPACE BLASTERS. *And teams stick together.*

Also, there was *no* way I was going to face a **zombie werewolf** all alone.[14]

---

[14] Even Spaceman Jack would be afraid of a zombie werewolf.

Katie and Kevin are definitely <u>NOT</u> afraid of answering some author questions ❗❕

So, we've <u>TOTALLY</u> read the second of Sam's adventures *Sam Wu is NOT Afraid of Sharks* now, do you think he is feeling any braver these days?

Sam is ALWAYS as brave as he can be, but we think the more adventures he faces, the braver he gets.

I love Sam's shark facts - especially that they have 8 senses! If you could have an extra sense - or two! - what would it be?

Kevin: I would like to sense when there are cupcakes nearby. A special cupcake sense.

Katie: I grew up in California, so I would want to be able to sense earthquakes before they happen!

Crazy Charlie might be the best name for a shark we have EVER heard! Did you have any pets with crazy names? Obviously hopefully not sharks . . .

Kevin: I once had a pet goldfish named Sebastian. But if I had a cat I'd name him Walter the Pagemaster.

Katie: I had a dog named Daisy, which was funny because she was HUGE dog. And my brother had a Rosy Boa named Rosie. Rosie the Rosy Boa was actually the inspiration for Fang!

Have you ever swum with sharks?

Kevin: Only in my dreams – and it was terrifying!

Katie: Not that I know of . . . but sharks are sneaky so maybe I have and just didn't see them! I would love to go swimming with Whale Sharks one day – they are gentle giants.

We loved the sound of Ralph & Regina's Beach Birthday Bash (aka shark attack take 2). Where would you have your ideal party?

Katie: Just like Ralph and Regina, I love the beach! I had lots of my birthday parties at the beach growing up and it is my favorite place for a party.

Kevin: I would want to have my birthday party in a huge bouncy castle in outer space !//!

ACKNOWLEDGEMENTS

We love writing Sam Wu – but we couldn't have made it into a real book that you can hold in your hands without the help and support of some amazing people!

If we had our own space ship on Space Blasters, our captain would be Claire Wilson, our fearless agent who always guides us in the right direction. Thank you for believing in us and believing in Sam Wu.

We are tremendously grateful to everyone at Egmont for supporting Sam Wu! Thank you to our whole team of brilliant editors – Ali Dougal, Emily Sharratt, Rachel Mann, Rebecca Lewis-Oakes and Lindsey Heaven. We've loved working with all of you.

Huge thank you to our incredibly talented illustrator Nathan Reed for bringing Sam and his friends to life on the page! The illustrations are our favorite part of the book.

Thank you as well to genius designers Sam Perrett and Lizzie Gardiner who made the pages look so awesome, to Olivia Carson in marketing, our publicist Siobhan McDermott, and everyone else at Egmont who worked on the book. We are so happy Sam Wu has found such a great home at Egmont.

We'd like to thank our families and friends for all their support and excitement. Special thank you to our grandparents: Mimi, Pop-Pop, Grandpa Bob, and Po-Po. And huge thanks and love to Katie's siblings: Jack and Jane, Kevin's sister, Stephanie, and our brother- and sister-in-law, Ben and Cat.

And thank you to our parents, for everything.

No night light needed here because...

SAM WU is <u>NOT</u> afraid of the **DARK**

I am totally OKAY!!! with this!

KATIE & KEVIN TSANG
Illustrated by Nathan Reed

Out February 2019!

Sam Wu is TOTALLY okay camping in the woods with his friends and cousin Stanley. What could *possibly* go wrong?

EGMONT